The New Baby at Your House

The New Baby

BY JOANNA COLE

REVISED EDITION

PHOTOGRAPHS BY MARGARET MILLER

MORROW JUNIOR BOOKS / NEW YORK

at Your House

The author would like to thank
Louise Bates Ames, co-director of the Gesell Institute for Human Development,
and Daisy Edmondson, former senior editor of *Parents* magazine,
for reading and suggesting changes in the manuscript for this book.
Thanks also to Margo Rideout for asking for a book that tells *all* sides to having a new sibling.

The photographer would like to thank all of the families who appear in this book
for their extraordinary generosity and patience: Andrew, Luz, Alexa, and Brittany Correa; Bobbi,
Summer, and Matt Flowers; Billy and Timmy Ford; Steven, Lory, Amos, Charlie, and Joel Goldstein;
Robyn and Max Greenberg; Luis Jackson; Carson Leydecker; Emily Queen; James, Lesa, Jamie, and
Malcolm Ransome; Travis and Rachel Reuther; Rachel and Craig Simmons; Siri, Eve,
and Simone Teitelbaum; and Chris, Sharon, Kelli, and Christopher VanHouten.

The text type is 16-point Lucida Sans Roman.

Published by Morrow Junior Books
a division of William Morrow and Company, Inc.
1350 Avenue of the Americas, New York, NY 10019
www.williammorrow.com

Printed in Hong Kong by South China Printing Company (1988) Ltd.

1 2 3 4 5 6 7 8 9 10

Library of Congress Cataloging-in-Publication Data
Cole, Joanna.
The new baby at your house/Joanna Cole; photographs by Margaret Miller.—Rev. ed.
p. cm.
Includes bibliographical references.
Summary: Describes the activities and changes involved in having a new baby in the house and the feelings
experienced by the older brothers and sisters.
ISBN 0-688-13897-7 (trade)—ISBN 0-688-13898-5 (library)
1. Infants—Juvenile literature.   2. Brothers and sisters—Juvenile literature.   [1. Babies.   2. Brothers and sisters.]
I. Miller, Margaret, date, ill.   II. Title.   HQ774.C58 1998   306.875—dc21   97-29267   CIP AC

A NOTE TO PARENTS

When a new baby is born in a family, it is natural for an older sibling to have all kinds of feelings. One child may be proud of being a big sister. Another may be worried that he will be displaced by the newcomer. Yet another may seem too busy with her own life to have much interest in the new baby. Whatever a child's dominant feeling, however, it is likely that others are there, too. A child may have negative feelings or worries that he tries to keep hidden. Or she may feel different things at different times: loving one moment, competitive the next, angry at her parents for the whole situation.

A parent's job is not to "fix things" so the negative feelings will go away and everyone will be happy all the time. Children don't need to be protected from the realization that their parents can love and care for another child. But they do need time to adjust to a new situation. And they need to have their feelings acknowledged and to feel included in the family.

The first way to include the older child or children in the family is to *prepare* them for the arrival of the new baby. Keeping a first child in the dark about the expected baby is unfair. Children under three probably shouldn't be told right away, because their sense of time is so limited that they can't comprehend an event that will take place eight months hence. Nevertheless, it is important to tell a small child about the baby by the time the pregnancy shows, before he learns it from others. If a child senses that a secret is being kept from him, he begins the relationship to his sibling with a feeling of being left out.

It is also considerate to include older children in some of the activities during the pregnancy. For instance, they can come along on a visit to the obstetrician and hear the baby's heartbeat.

In preparing for the arrival, it is helpful to talk about the baby. But it is not advisable to make false promises, such as "The baby will be someone for you to play with." Such a promise is bound to end up disappointing an older sibling, because, at first, the baby will do little else but eat, cry, and sleep. The best course is to be truthful and realistic about what it is like to have a baby in the house. One way to do this is to read this book with your child and to visit some families that have newborns.

Sometimes a child may withdraw or simply may not want to talk about the baby. If this happens, don't force your child to talk about it, and don't tell her how you think she "really" feels. But do let her know you are available, saying, "I'll be glad to answer any questions you may have about the baby" or "Some children have worries when a new baby is coming. If you have any, you can tell me about them." Often young children "talk about" their feelings in play, rather than in words. Ordinary play can help a child express herself, especially if you provide a family of dolls that includes parents, an older child, and a baby.

Most childcare experts advise against scheduling a lot of changes immediately before or after the birth, especially for toddlers and young children. Adjusting to the baby will be change enough. If you can help it, avoid such transitions as starting nursery school, hiring a new sitter, graduating from a crib to a bed, or learning to use the toilet. These events should happen well before the baby is due or be postponed until later.

As the birth approaches, a child needs to know exactly what will happen when the baby is born. Although some babies will be born at home, the vast majority of children will be separated from their mother for a few days while she is at a hospital or childbirth center. In this case, the child needs to be told that his mother will be away for a few days, where she will be, and what arrangements have been made for him. Experts say that it's usually best for

the older child to stay at home in familiar surroundings with people who have cared for him before. The ideal arrangement may be for the father to take time off from work and stay with the child.

Separation from parents is difficult, and the younger the child, the more difficult it will be. Experts urge parents to say good-bye to their children before they leave for the hospital, even if it means waking them up to do so. They may cry, but they will feel more secure if they know what is happening and do not wake up to find you gone.

Contact with the mother while she is away is essential. Studies have shown that children who are able to visit their mothers in the hospital make a better adjustment to the new baby than others, even if they appear very upset at parting. If the hospital resists the idea of a visit, perhaps your doctor or midwife can intercede for you.

Even if your child is not able to visit, frequent phone conversations will ease the separation. Talk about the baby a bit, but remember that your first child is more interested in *you* than the baby, and she needs attention from you. So most of the conversation should be about what is happening at home and acknowledgment that she misses you, and that you miss her.

Many families report that older siblings benefit from coming along when mother and baby leave the hospital, even if children are required to stay in the reception area with a friend or relative. The fact that you want your child there and spend time paying attention to him will reassure him about his importance to you.

Once at home, follow your child's lead as to whether she wants to look at the baby or just spend time with you. At some point, however, encourage her to inspect the baby and to help with feeding, bathing, and changing. Let her touch and hold the baby while sitting safely in an armchair.

With toddlers, feelings will change from positive to negative very quickly, and young children are more likely to express these feelings through actions than words. Therefore, toddlers should never be left alone with a baby. Stay close and be prepared to intercept any inappropriate moves physically.

Teach your child in a positive way that gentleness is the rule with babies. Avoid the words "don't" and "no" as much as possible. Instead, say encouraging things like "Be gentle; that's right" and "I like the way you hold her so carefully."

An older sibling is usually delighted when the baby responds to him in any way, such as watching his face, squeezing a finger, turning the head in response to a stroke on the cheek. When parents make a point of mentioning this responsiveness, it seems to help a child develop a loving feeling for the baby. One mother told me, "I always said to Christopher, 'Brian loves you' and 'He is happy when you talk to him.' Now that Brian is almost two, they get along very well most of the time."

When the baby becomes mobile, older siblings often feel their territory is being invaded. Children are not really able to work out problems like these on their own. They need help from their parents to find ways of protecting their toys and space. At other times, parents can show children how to include the baby in games. And they can be most helpful by explaining babies' behavior— for instance, babies grab toys because they are curious; babies want to be near big sisters and brothers because they love them—and by showing that babies can be distracted easily if they are offered a different toy or activity.

From the time they first find out about the baby until they must cope with a tag-along toddler, older brothers and sisters have several needs. They need regular time alone with both mother and father, time when they are the center of attention and love. They need help from parents to control their aggressive impulses toward the younger child. They need a chance to express sad, angry, or jealous feelings (not to be confused with aggressive *actions*). And they need to have their parents accept these feelings without trying to explain them away.

Most of all, children need to be reassured through words and actions that the arrival of the baby does not mean they have been replaced. Show your child that she can be loved and attended to in the presence of the baby. That he can be included in caring for and playing with the baby. And that she will always be an important, unique person in the family, no matter how large it may be.

FURTHER READING FOR PARENTS

From One Child to Two: What to Expect, How to Cope, and How to Enjoy Your Growing Family, by Judy Dunn. New York: Fawcett, 1995. The author is distinguished professor of human development at Pennsylvania State University, and she tells all you need to know about preparing your first child for the new baby. Very good at helping you understand how toddlers express their feelings and advising you on how to deal with regression and other difficult behaviors.

He Hit Me First: When Brothers and Sisters Fight, by Louise Bates Ames and others. New York: Warner Books, 1989. A realistic book about sibling rivalry by the well-known authority on child development. The book contains an especially good chapter on the arrival of a new baby, as well as a discussion of how much sibling rivalry is to be expected and how to cope with daily life in the family.

Loving Each One Best: A Caring and Practical Approach to Raising Siblings, by Nancy Samalin and Catherine Whitney. New York: Bantam, 1996. Based on the authors' experience conducting parenting workshops, this book is especially valuable for its advice on avoiding "the fairness trap"—the authors suggest responding to each child's special needs, rather than trying to treat both children exactly the same.

Surviving Sibling Rivalry, by Lee Canter and Marlene Canter. Santa Monica, CA: Lee Canter & Associates, 1993. A very practical and down-to-earth book by two experienced parenting counselors. The open format packs a lot of advice into a brief and user-friendly package.

Welcoming Your Second Baby, by Vicki Lansky. Deephaven, MN: The Book Peddlers, 1990. Part of the author's "Practical Parenting" series, this fast-reading book combines basic advice with quotes from parents who've "been there." It's hard to think of any issue about the new baby that isn't covered here with brevity and wisdom.

Your Second Child: A Guide for Parents, by Joan Solomon Weiss. New York: Summit Books, 1981. A well-researched look at the decision to have a second child, the effect of birth order on a child's personality, and recommended ways of handling sibling rivalry.

Lots of families have new babies. There's a new baby at Molly's house. There's one at Michael's, too. Is there a new baby at *your* house?

Sara knows a baby will be born soon. That's because Sara's mother is pregnant. The baby is inside her body, in a special place called her womb, or uterus. Sara can feel the baby moving and kicking.

Julie's mother is pregnant, too. Julie likes to pretend that the baby can understand when she talks. She asks the baby all kinds of questions, such as, "Are you warm in there?" or "Would you like some cornflakes?"

Just before a baby is born, most mothers go to the hospital. Sara helped her mommy pack a going-away bag.

Sara had to stay home. But Mommy called her on the phone. "I love you, Sara," said Mommy.

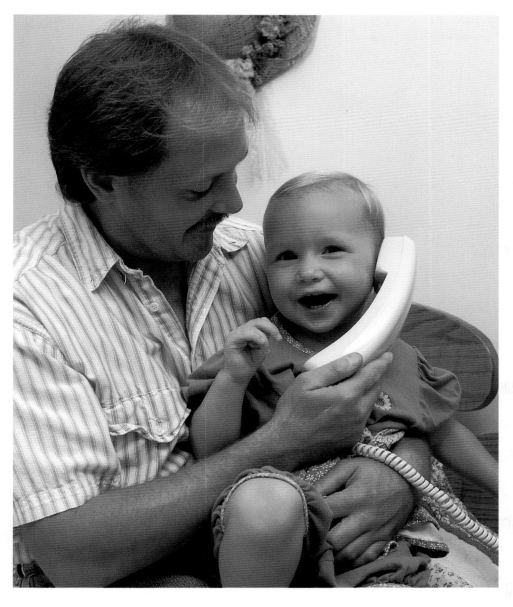

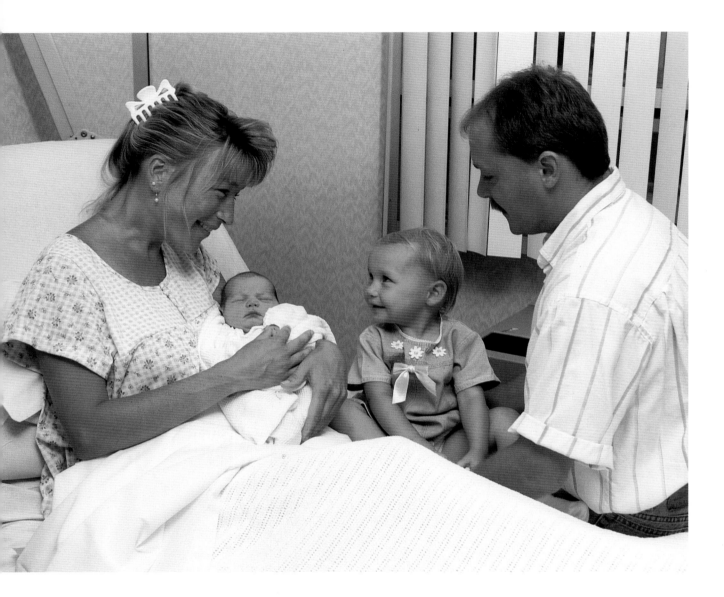

Later, Daddy took Sara to visit the hospital. She hugged her mother and got her first look at Tyler, her new baby brother.

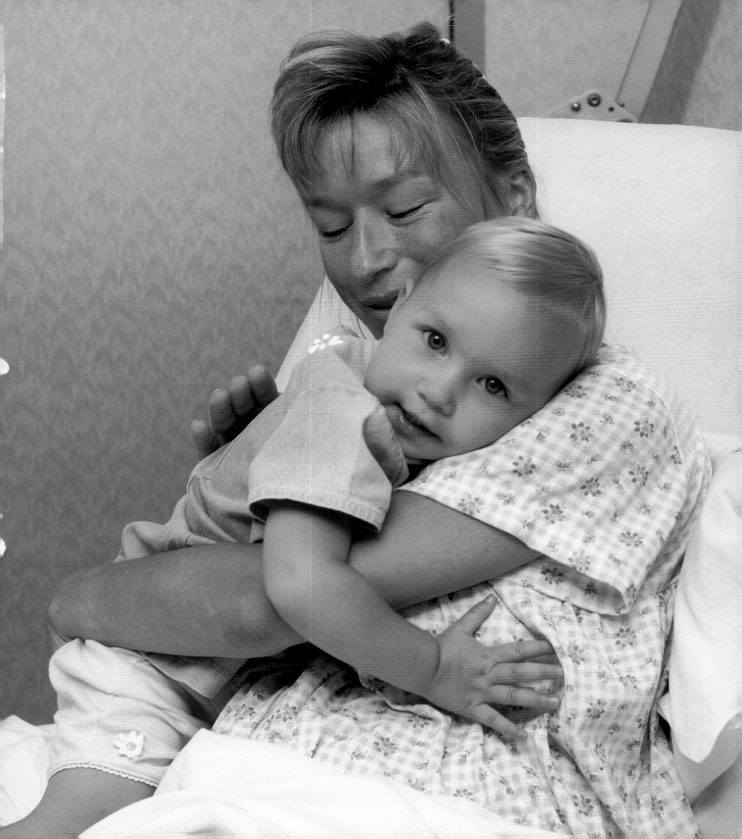

At home, Michael looked closely at his baby brother, Peter. He was amazed at how little Peter was. "Look at his tiny toes!" Michael exclaimed.

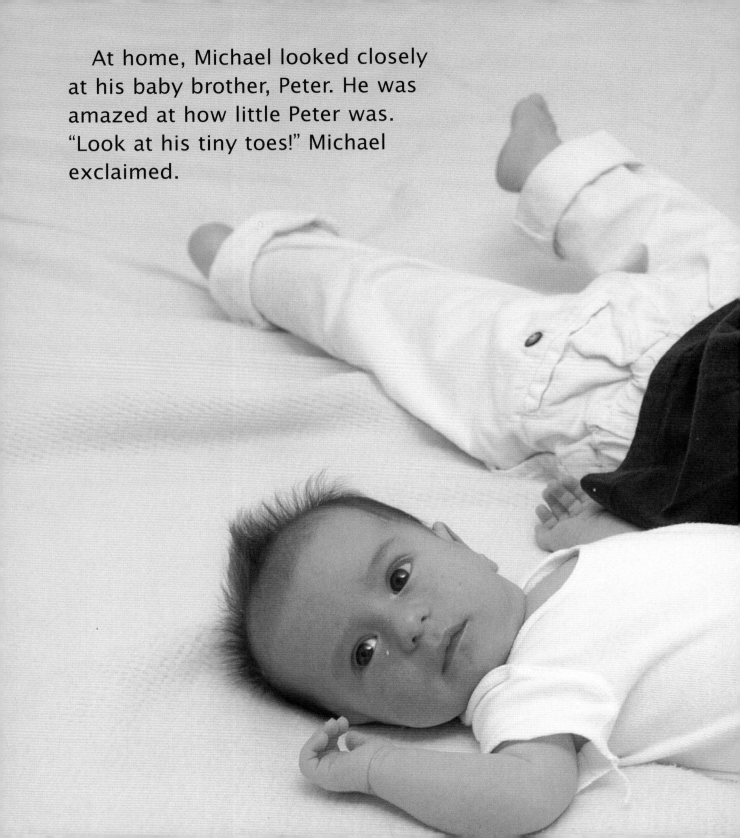

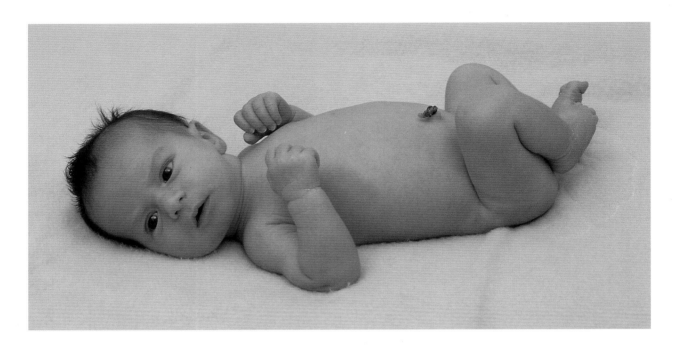

Julie noticed that a piece of the umbilical cord was still attached to Laura's belly. All new babies have this. You did, too, when you were born.

After a while, the cord will dry up and fall off. Only a little scab will be left. When the scab heals, it will leave a navel, or belly button, just like yours.

Newborn babies are not strong. They cannot even lift up their heads. We have to be careful with babies.

Even though new babies are small and weak, they can still do many things. As soon as they are born, they can see, hear, taste, smell, feel, and cry. (Did you know that at first babies don't shed tears when they cry? These will come later.)

What else can new babies do? They are born knowing how to suck milk from their mother's breast or from a bottle.

Babies get all the nourishment they need from milk. It will be a while before they are ready to eat solid food.

Very young babies can also grip tightly with their little hands. Baby Laura gave her big sister's finger a good hard squeeze.

If you stroke your baby's palm gently, the baby might grip your finger, too.

Babies like to look at things. Sometimes Julie moves a toy back and forth in front of Laura. Laura's eyes follow the toy.

You can try this, too. If your brother or sister looks away, it means the baby is tired of looking and needs a rest.

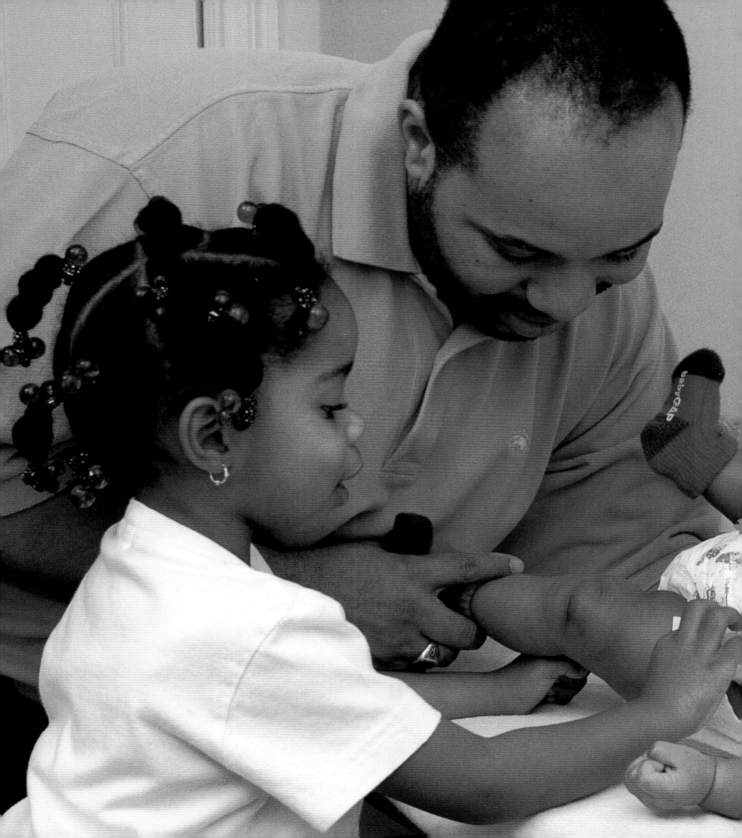

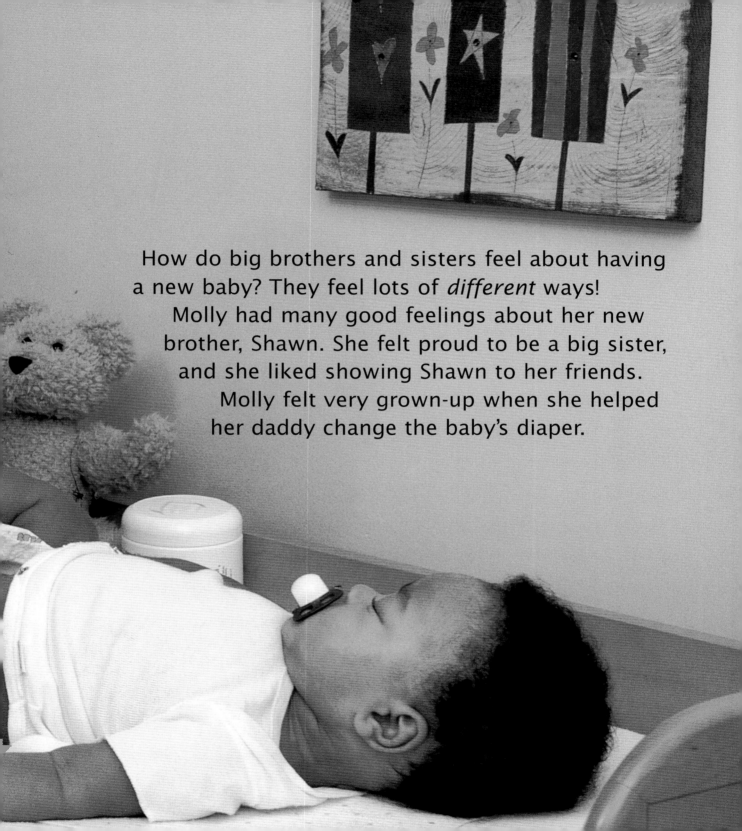

How do big brothers and sisters feel about having a new baby? They feel lots of *different* ways! Molly had many good feelings about her new brother, Shawn. She felt proud to be a big sister, and she liked showing Shawn to her friends. Molly felt very grown-up when she helped her daddy change the baby's diaper.

But naturally, Molly had some not-so-good feelings, too. When Shawn cried, Molly covered her ears. "Can't you make him stop?" she asked her mother.

Molly's mother explained, "Babies have to cry. That is how they tell us they need something."

Molly understood, but she still didn't like it when the baby cried.

Sometimes Molly felt left out when her parents took care of Shawn. She wished *she* could be the baby and get all the attention. Do you ever feel this way, too?

Michael wanted his daddy to play with him "right now!" He was angry because he had to wait until the baby was finished with his bottle. "I don't want a brother anymore," Michael said. "Take him back!"

Once Michael wanted to poke the baby, but his daddy wouldn't let him. "It's okay to be mad," said Daddy, "but I can't let you hurt the baby."

Michael said his feelings about the baby were "all mixed up." Sometimes he loved baby Peter. But other times he got mad. Daddy made Michael pick up his toys, but Peter never had to do any chores.

Do you ever have mixed-up feelings like these? It's okay to have a lot of feelings when a baby is born in your family.

Michael even worried that his mommy and daddy didn't love him anymore. "All you do is take care of the baby," he complained.

"Taking care of a baby does take a lot of time," said Mommy. "But we will never stop loving you!"

"You are very special to us," said Daddy. Then Mommy and Daddy held Michael in their arms and hugged him tight.

Big kids can do lots of things babies can't do. A baby needs to be changed. You can learn to use the toilet. Babies drink milk. You can eat more exciting things—like ice cream. You have interesting toys and lots of friends. It's fun to be big!

When you are big, you learn to do hard things. You know how to do a good job. Mommy and Daddy are proud of you. They like to see you growing up.

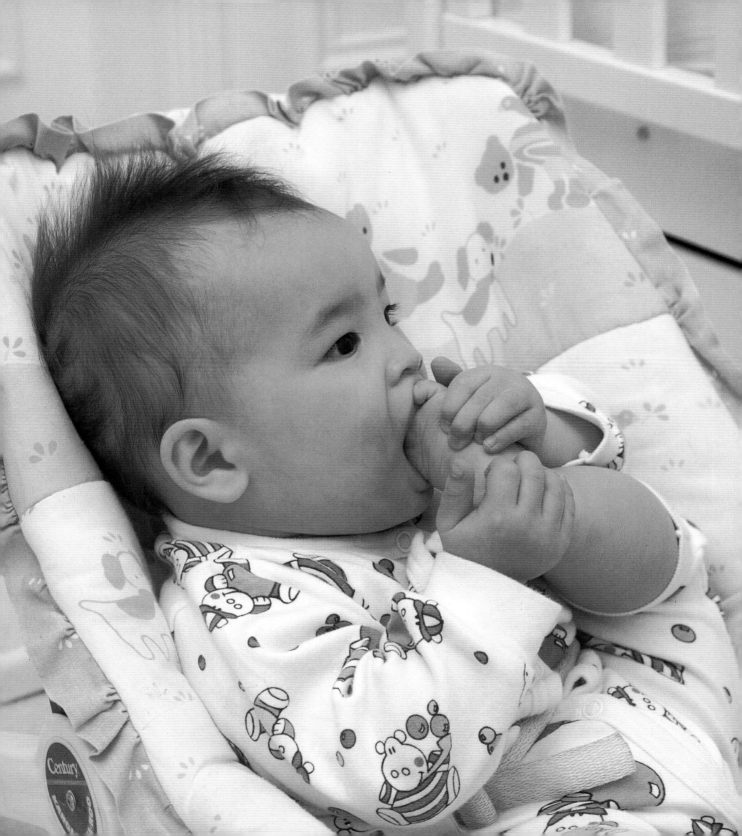

You can watch your baby brother or sister grow up, too.

Every day, babies seem to get bigger. They get more hair, and teeth start poking their way out of their gums.

Babies learn to grab things, and they put everything in their mouth—even their feet!

At first babies can't smile and laugh. But before long they learn how. Stevie laughs most when his big brother, Ben, makes funny faces.

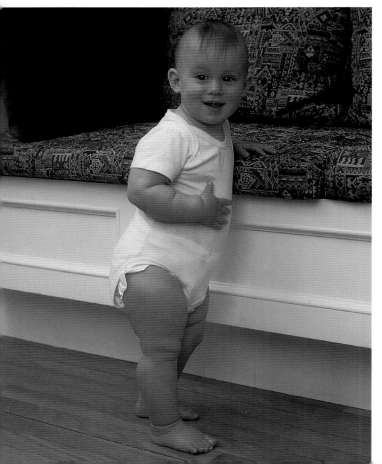

Before they can walk, babies learn to sit up... crawl...and stand.

As babies grow, they even learn to play games. Jessica had fun playing peekaboo with her little sister, Hannah.

What else happens when babies grow? They learn to get into trouble! Jessica was upset when Hannah knocked over her blocks.

Mommy and Daddy put Jessica's special things up high to keep them safe from the baby. But it didn't always help! Baby Hannah loved her big sister and wanted to do everything Jessica did.

It can be hard when there are two kids and only *one* dalmatian! But some games are much more fun with a brother or sister.

You are different from your sister or brother. You have your own ideas, your own feelings, and your own way of doing things.

Your parents love you as you are. They love you because you are special. You are the only *you* in the whole world.

When a family grows, love grows, too. Julie knows that in her family, love can get as big as it has to.
Isn't your family like that, too?